BOOK
1
I
VOLUME

PROLOGUE

Without any warning, passengers on an airborne Boeing 747 mysteriously disappear from their seats. Nothing remains except rumpled piles of clothing, jewelry, dental fillings, surgical pins, and the like. All over the world, in a flash, cars are left unmanned. Terror and chaos reign worldwide as the cataclysm unfolds. For those left behind, the apocalypse has just begun.

EFT BEHIND® BOOK 1 VOL I
apted from the original Tim LaHaye and Jerry B. Jenkins novels. Story Adaptation John S. Layman Pencils Aaron Lopresti Ink Randy Emberlin
lors WildStorm FX Letters Jenna Garcia Creative Director Jim Bolton Cover Direction & Design Rule29 Editor Neal Pozner
blished by Tyndale House Publishers, Inc.

KEY CHARACTERS

Your center for info on who's who as the Left Behind Graphic Novel series continues.

BUCK WILLIAMS

Star reporter for the *Global Weekly* news magazine, Buck has witnessed many amazing and unbelievable events. Still, nothing in his career as a journalist has prepared him for this...

RAYFORD STEELE

A pilot for Pan-Continental Airlines, Rayford is about to embark on the most unforgettable journey of all.

HATTIE DURHAM

A flight attendant for Pan-Continental, and a friend to Rayford Steele; perhaps one of them is looking for something more than friendship?

THE STEELE FAMILY: RAYFORD, IRENE, RAY JR., AND CHLOE

A loyal churchgoer with a strong belief that the Rapture is imminent, Irene's devotion has repeatedly been a source of contention between Rayford and her. Young son Ray Jr. is caught in between, while daughter Chloe attends college on the West Coast.

CHAIM ROSENZWEIG

Nobel Prize–winning chemist and inventor of a biological formula that changed the face of Israel.

IT'LL BE MORNING BEFORE YOU KNOW IT, CHRIS. WE GOT REPORTS OF CLEAR SKIES--NO TURBULENCE, NO INCLEMENT WEATHER-- ALL THE WAY TO LONDON. THIS FLIGHT SHOULD BE A CAKEWALK...

...IF ONLY *EVERY* FLIGHT COULD GO THIS SMOOTHLY.

ROGER THAT, CAPTAIN.

AND LET'S HOPE OUR RETURN TRIP TO CHICAGO GOES JUST AS WELL.

SO, CAPTAIN... ANY BIG PLANS FOR OUR LAYOVER IN MERRY OL' ENGLAND?

YOU KNOW, CHRIS, NOW THAT YOU MENTION IT...I HAVE HAD AN *IDEA* OR TWO....

KNOCK KNOCK

I HOPE YOU'RE DECENT!

I THOUGHT YOU BOYS COULD USE A MID-FLIGHT PICK-ME-UP.

EVERYTHING OKAY BACK THERE?

I THINK EVERYBODY HAS SETTLED IN PRETTY WELL. I'LL BE MAKING ANOTHER ROUND OR SO, AND THEN I THINK MOST PEOPLE WILL BE DOZING OFF.

JUST GIVE ME A HOLLER IF YOU NEED ANYTHING, RAYFORD...

WHY, HATTIE DURHAM, YOU READ MY MIND!

JUST WHAT THE DOCTOR ORDERED, HATTIE. MUCH OBLIGED.

...ANYTHING AT ALL.

IT'S GOOD TO KNOW YOU'RE SO... *CONSCIENTIOUS*... HATTIE. I'D SAY THIS BIRD'S IN GOOD HANDS WITH YOU LOOKIN' OUT FOR US.

WELL, CAPTAIN, I AIM TO PLEASE.

HA HA! WELL, YOU WON'T BE HEARING ANY COMPLAINTS FROM ME!

CIAO, BOYS!

≥SIGH≤

WHAT?!?

I HOPE OUR LOVELY SENIOR FLIGHT ATTENDANT DOESN'T HAVE ANYTHING TO DO WITH THESE *"IDEAS"* YOU'RE HAVING.

HATTIE'S A GREAT-LOOKING LADY, THAT'S FOR SURE...

LAST I HEARD, CAPTAIN RAYFORD STEELE WAS A HAPPILY MARRIED MAN, WITH A HOUSE IN THE SUBURBS AND TWO TERRIFIC KIDS.

YOU ARE STILL *HAPPILY* MARRIED... RIGHT?

WELL...I...UH...I'M NOT EXACTLY *UN*HAPPY, BUT LATELY...LATELY...

MY WIFE SPENDS AN *AWFUL* LOT OF TIME AT CHURCH, CHRIS.

"FOR THE LONGEST TIME, I JUST THOUGHT IT WAS A PHASE IRENE WAS GOING THROUGH... LIKE WHEN SHE GOT INTO AMWAY, OR TUPPERWARE, OR AEROBICS.

STEELE

"WE'D GONE TO CHURCH FAIRLY REGULARLY AS A FAMILY, THE FOUR OF US --IRENE, CHLOE, RAY JR. AND ME...

"AND I DIDN'T MIND GOING *ONCE IN A WHILE*, BUT ONCE CHLOE LEFT FOR COLLEGE IRENE BECAME, I DON'T KNOW... *FANATICAL*.

"IT WAS LIKE SHE GOT HOOKED, JOINING UP WITH A SMALLER CONGREGATION, GOING TO WEEKLY BIBLE STUDY, ATTENDING CHURCH *EVERY* SUNDAY.

"SHE GOT MORE AND MORE OBSESSED, AND, FRANKLY, I GREW LESS AND LESS INTERESTED.

NEW HOPE VILLAGE CHURCH

"IT GOT TO BE WHERE RELIGION WAS *ALL* SHE COULD TALK ABOUT.

"ON AND ON ABOUT JESUS' LOVE...

"...THE SALVATION OF SOULS...

"...AND HER FAVORITE SUBJECT OF ALL: THE END OF THE WORLD.

"LATELY SHE'D BEEN READING EVERYTHING SHE COULD ABOUT THE RAPTURE OF THE CHURCH."

CAN YOU IMAGINE, RAFE? *JESUS* COMING TO GET US BEFORE WE DIE?

YEAH. BOY, THAT WOULD JUST KILL ME.

IF I DIDN'T KNOW WHAT WOULD HAPPEN TO ME, I WOULDN'T BE SO GLIB.

I *DO* KNOW WHAT WOULD HAPPEN TO ME.

I'D BE DEAD, GONE, *FINIS.* BUT *YOU,* OF COURSE, WOULD FLY RIGHT UP TO HEAVEN.

COME ON, IRENE. TELL ME THOUSANDS WOULDN'T JUST KEEL OVER IF THEY SAW JESUS COMING BACK FOR ALL THE GOOD PEOPLE.

IF IT MAKES YOU FEEL ANY BETTER, I'M HAPPY THAT YOU CAN BE SO COCKSURE.

I'VE TOLD YOU AND TOLD YOU. *SAVED* PEOPLE AREN'T GOOD PEOPLE, THEY'RE JUST...

I KNOW, I KNOW...JUST *FORGIVEN.*

I ONLY BELIEVE WHAT THE BIBLE SAYS.

GOOD FOR YOU.

"SEEMS LIKE WE'VE HAD A LOT OF FIGHTS ABOUT THIS LATELY."

WE HAD A FIGHT ABOUT IT JUST BEFORE I LEFT FOR THIS FLIGHT.

BUT STILL, YOU'RE A FAITHFUL HUSBAND, RIGHT?

OF *COURSE* I'M A FAITHFUL HUSBAND!

ENOUGH OF THIS CHIT-CHAT, SMITH. WHY DON'T YOU TRY AND GET A BIT OF SHUT-EYE?

I MEAN, AS FAITHFUL AS THE NEXT GUY, ANYWAY.

AYE AYE, CAPTAIN.

WELL, I GUESS IT ALL STARTS WITH CHAIM ROSENZWEIG, AND IF EVER THERE'S A GUY WHO DOESN'T NEED AN INTRODUCTION, IT'S HIM.

GLOBAL *WEEKLY'S* NEWS-MAKER OF THE YEAR LAST YEAR!

THAT'S RIGHT. NOT TO MENTION *TIME'S* "MAN OF THE YEAR." FIRST TIME ANYBODY HAS GOTTEN BOTH IN THE SAME YEAR.

I'VE MET THE GUY. SWEETEST MAN YOU'D EVER HAVE THE PLEASURE TO CALL A FRIEND.

STILL HUMBLE ENOUGH TO CALL HIMSELF A "BOTANIST," THOUGH IN TRUTH, HE'S A *GENIUS* CHEMICAL ENGINEER...

..."AND WHEN IT CAME TIME TO VOTE FOR THAT NOBEL PRIZE, IT DIDN'T TAKE ANYBODY VERY LONG TO FIGURE OUT THIS MAN WAS A SHOO-IN.

"'IRRIGATION HAS NOT BEEN A PROBLEM FOR DECADES,' CHAIM MAINTAINED, 'BUT ALL THAT DID WAS MAKE THE SAND WET. MY FORMULA, ADDED TO THE WATER, FERTILIZES THE LAND!'

"THAT SYNTHETIC FORMULA OF HIS CAUSED THE DESERT SANDS OF ISRAEL TO BLOOM LIKE A GREENHOUSE. EVERY INCH OF GROUND BLOSSOMED WITH FLOWERS AND GRAINS, INCLUDING PRODUCE NEVER BEFORE CONCEIVABLE IN ISRAEL.

"ALMOST INSTANTANEOUSLY ISRAEL BECAME ONE OF THE WEALTHIEST NATIONS OF EARTH...

"...NOT TO MENTION THE MOST ENVIED, SINCE ROSENZWEIG--AND ISRAEL-- HAVE THUS FAR DECLINED TO SHARE THE FORMULA.

"THE PROSPERITY BROUGHT ABOUT BY THE MIRACLE FORMULA LITERALLY CHANGED THE COURSE OF HISTORY FOR ISRAEL.

"NEEDLESS TO SAY, WHEN MY EDITOR STEVE PLANK OFFERED ME A CHANCE TO INTERVIEW THE GREAT MAN, I JUMPED FOR IT.

"AFTER ALL, CHAIM ROSENZWEIG IS ONE OF THE MOST HONORED AND REVERED MEN IN THE WORLD...

"...SOUGHT AFTER BY GLOBAL LEADERS, AND PROTECTED BY SECURITY SYSTEMS AS COMPLEX AS THOSE THAT PROTECT HEADS OF STATE.

"UPON ARRIVAL, I WAS MET BY AN ARMED GARRISON THAT WOULD PROVIDE MY ESCORT.

"THEY LED ME TO A MILITARY COMPOUND, IN A KIBBUTZ ON THE OUTSKIRTS OF HAIFA.

"ISRAELI LEADERS WERE NOT STUPID, AFTER ALL. A KIDNAPPED AND TORTURED ROSENZWEIG COULD BE FORCED TO REVEAL A SECRET THAT WOULD SIMILARLY REVOLUTIONIZE ANY NATION IN THE WORLD.

"BUT DESPITE THE CAUTIOUS, PROTECTIVE ATMOSPHERE, ROSENZWEIG HIMSELF PROVED TO BE A VERY WARM AND OPEN MAN.

"WE BECAME FAST FRIENDS.

"BUT NOT EVERYBODY WAS SO ENAMORED WITH DR. ROSENZWEIG AND THE ISRAELI GOVERNMENT.

"RUSSIA THOUGHT ROSENZWEIG'S FORMULA WAS THE KEY TO RESURRECTING ITS MASSIVE NATION FOLLOWING THE SHATTERING OF THE UNION OF SOVIET SOCIALIST REPUBLICS.

"IMAGINE WHAT THE FORMULA MIGHT DO IF MODIFIED TO WORK ON THE VAST TUNDRA OF RUSSIA!

"WHEN THE WORLD ECONOMIES STREAMLINED INTO THREE CURRENCIES--DOLLARS, MARKS, AND YEN--THE TRANSITION WAS NOT AN EASY ONE FOR RUSSIA.

"THE COUNTRY HAD BECOME A GREAT BROODING GIANT WITH A DEVASTATED ECONOMY AND REGRESSED TECHNOLOGY.

"ALL THE NATION HAD WAS MILITARY MIGHT, EVERY SPARE MARK GOING INTO WEAPONRY.

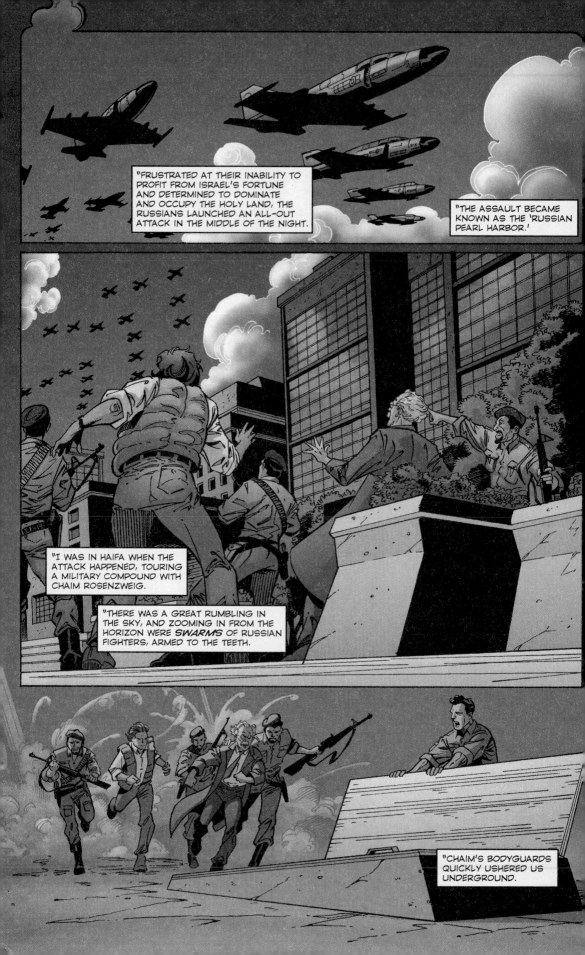

"FRUSTRATED AT THEIR INABILITY TO PROFIT FROM ISRAEL'S FORTUNE AND DETERMINED TO DOMINATE AND OCCUPY THE HOLY LAND, THE RUSSIANS LAUNCHED AN ALL-OUT ATTACK IN THE MIDDLE OF THE NIGHT.

"THE ASSAULT BECAME KNOWN AS THE 'RUSSIAN PEARL HARBOR.'

"I WAS IN HAIFA WHEN THE ATTACK HAPPENED, TOURING A MILITARY COMPOUND WITH CHAIM ROSENZWEIG.

"THERE WAS A GREAT RUMBLING IN THE SKY, AND ZOOMING IN FROM THE HORIZON WERE *SWARMS* OF RUSSIAN FIGHTERS, ARMED TO THE TEETH.

"CHAIM'S BODYGUARDS QUICKLY USHERED US UNDERGROUND.

"THIS WAS NO GRANDSTAND PLAY TO BRING ISRAEL TO ITS KNEES.

"RUSSIA SENT EVERYTHING IT HAD--INTERCONTINENTAL MISSILES AND NUCLEAR-EQUIPPED MIG FIGHTER-BOMBERS

"I SAW THE RADAR SCREEN AND FIGURED THE END WAS NEAR.

"THEIR MISSION WAS CLEAR: *TOTAL ANNIHILATION*.

"ISRAELI DEFENSE OR NO, A VOLLEY OF THIS MUCH PURE FIREPOWER WOULD UNDOUBTEDLY BRING ABOUT ISRAEL'S VIRTUAL DISAPPEARANCE FROM THE FACE OF THE EARTH.

"ALL SORTS OF THINGS RUSHED THROUGH MY HEAD...

"WHY HAD I NEVER MARRIED? WOULD THERE BE REMNANTS OF MY BODY FOR MY FATHER AND BROTHER TO IDENTIFY?

"*WAS* THERE A GOD? WOULD DEATH BE THE END?

"A FEW MINUTES INTO THE HOLOCAUST, THE ROOM QUAKING FROM EXPLOSIONS ALL AROUND US, I FIGURED I'D BE NO MORE DEAD OUTSIDE THAN IN.

"NOBODY ELSE WAS PAYING ATTENTION TO ME.

"SO I SLIPPED AWAY, DETERMINED TO BE THE *ONE* PERSON AT THIS POST WHO WOULD SEE AND KNOW WHAT KILLED HIM.

"YOU KNOW WHAT THE *REAL* KICKER WAS? NOT A *SINGLE* CASUALTY WAS REPORTED IN ALL OF ISRAEL.

"ANYTHING ATOMIC ERUPTED HIGH IN THE ATMOSPHERE.

"THE DOWNED FIGHTERS FELL BETWEEN BUILDINGS AND IN DESERTED STREETS OR FIELDS.

"ANCIENT WALLS WERE LEVELED, BUT THERE WAS NOT SO MUCH AS A *SCRATCH* ON *ANY* LIVING CREATURE IN ISRAEL.

"MISSILES SIMPLY *REFUSED* TO DETONATE.

"IT DIDN'T TAKE LONG FOR ISRAEL TO RETURN TO NORMAL...

"*BETTER* THAN NORMAL, REALLY, BECAUSE IN THE RUINS THE ISRAELIS FOUND A HIDDEN RESERVE OF FUEL.

THE COUNTRY COULD THRIVE LIKE NEVER BEFORE.

THANKS FOR SHARING YOUR STORY, MR. WILLIAMS. I HAPPEN TO THINK WHAT HAPPENED TO YOU WAS A GENUINE *MIRACLE* FROM GOD.

I'M GOING TO GET SOME SLEEP NOW. I'LL PROBABLY HAVE SOME PRETTY AMAZING DREAMS, TOO, AFTER TALKING TO YOU.

GOOD NIGHT TO YOU.

ZZZZZ

SIR, CAN I BRING YOU ANYTHING?

OH NO, THANK YOU. I'M OKAY.

SNNOOARK!!

WELL, *MOSTLY* OKAY.

EXCUSE ME!

OH!!!!

COULD YOU HELP ME? I'M FLYING WITH A FRIEND. I DOZED OFF A WHILE AGO, AND NOW SHE'S GONE.

SHE'S ACTUALLY BEEN GONE FOR A WHILE NOW, AND I'M AFRAID SHE MIGHT BE ILL.

SURE...I'D BE... HAPPY TO. PLEASE RETURN TO YOUR SEAT AND I'LL TRACK HER DOWN IN A JIFFY.

BUT YOU DIDN'T...

...YOU DIDN'T EVEN ASK WHAT SHE LOOKS LIKE!

THIS IS *CRAZY!* WHAT'S GOING ON HERE?

HELLO?

ANYBODY HOME?

VACANT

IT'S SOME KIND OF PRANK! IT'S GOTTA BE...

PEOPLE DON'T SIMPLY *DISAPPEAR.*

=SIGH=

RAYFORD, M'MAN... I SURE HOPE YOU KNOW WHAT YOU'RE DOING.

HATTIE.

I'VE BEEN THINKING... HOW WOULD YOU LIKE TO GO TO DINNER WITH ME?

SAY, HATTIE, LET'S GO TO DINNER, JUST YOU AND ME, WHAT DO YOU SAY?

HATTIE... ...WHAT WOULD YOU SAY TO US SPENDING A LITTLE TIME TOGETHER? LET'S SAY, OH, I DON'T KNOW-- DINNER?

YOU WOULD? OH, WELL, THAT'S JUST GREAT!

CAPTAIN STEELE!!

HATTIE!

HOLD ON A MINUTE, HATTIE. LISTEN TO WHAT YOU'RE SAYING. THIS IS *CRAZY!*

I KNOW IT IS! BUT I *KNOW* WHAT I SAW!

HATTIE, IT'S STILL DARK. WE'LL *FIND* THEM!

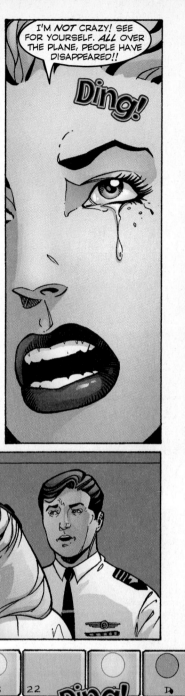

I'M *NOT* CRAZY! SEE FOR YOURSELF. *ALL* OVER THE PLANE, PEOPLE HAVE DISAPPEARED!!

Ding!

Ding!
Ding!
Ding!

SHOULD I TURN ON THE CABIN LIGHTS?

THE LESS PEOPLE KNOW RIGHT NOW THE BETTER.

IT LOOKS LIKE THE PASSENGERS ARE FIGURING IT OUT ON THEIR OWN JUST FINE.

Ding!
Ding!
Ding!
Ding!

YAWWWNNNN...

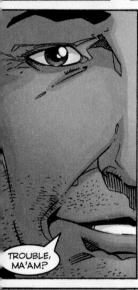

TROUBLE, MA'AM?

IT'S MY HAROLD.

DOES HE NEED SOMETHING?

HE'S *GONE!*

I'M SORRY?

HE'S DISAPPEARED!

WELL, I'M SURE HE SLIPPED OFF TO THE WASHROOM WHILE YOU WERE SLEEPING.

WOULD YOU MIND CHECKING FOR ME? AND TAKE A *BLANKET?*

I'M AFRAID HE'S GONE OFF NAKED.

HE'S A RELIGIOUS PERSON, AND HE'LL BE TERRIBLY EMBARRASSED.

Whummp!

WHOOPS... SORRY!

EXCUSE ME, BUT I'M *LOOKING* FOR SOMEONE...

YEAH, BUDDY? WHO *ISN'T?!?*

YOUR ATTENTION, PLEASE. I NEED YOU ALL TO RETURN TO YOUR SEATS AND FASTEN YOUR SEAT BELTS.

I'M LOOKING FOR--

EVERYBODY IS LOOKING FOR SOMEONE, SIR. WE HOPE TO HAVE SOME INFORMATION FOR YOU IN A FEW MINUTES.

NOW, PLEASE.

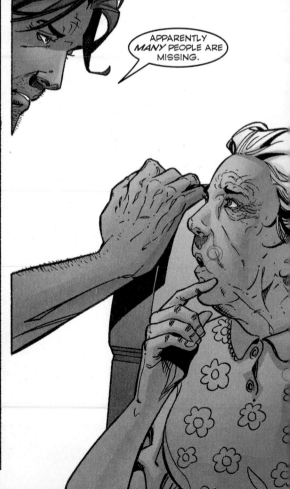

APPARENTLY *MANY* PEOPLE ARE MISSING.

MAN, AM I GLAD YOU'RE BACK, CAP'N. YOU WOULDN'T *BELIEVE* WHAT'S COMING OVER THE RADIO.

LET ME GUESS: MISSING PEOPLE, RIGHT?

WE'VE GOT MORE THAN A HUNDRED PEOPLE GONE WITH NOTHING BUT THEIR CLOTHES LEFT BEHIND.

MAYDAY, MAYDAY. THIS IS PAN-CONTINENTAL FOUR-ONE-SEVEN TO HEATHROW. WE'VE GOT A BIT OF A *SITUATION* HERE. ANYBODY OUT THERE, OVER?

THIS IS CONCORDE SIX-ELEVEN, PAN HEAVY, WE READ YOU.

HUH? HOW DID YOU...

WE'RE MISSING FIFTY, PAN HEAVY, AND YOU?

YOU'RE MISSING PASSENGERS *TOO?*

NOT JUST US. PEOPLE *EVERYWHERE* HAVE DISAPPEARED. ORLY [L]OST AIR-TRAFFIC CONTROLLERS AND GROUND CONTROLLERS. [S]OME PLANES HAVE LOST FLIGHT CREWS. PLANES DOWN OVER AND AT EVERY MAJOR AIRPORT.

SO THIS WAS A SPONTANEOUS THING?

EVERYWHERE AT ONCE, JUST UNDER AN HOUR AGO.

UH... YOU GOT ANY IDEA ABOUT THIS?

NOT A BLESSED THING, CONCORDE.

GOOD CHOICE OF WORDS, PAN HEAVY, ACCORDING TO WHAT A LOT OF PEOPLE ARE SAYING...

LADIES AND GENTLEMEN. WE'RE NOT GOING TO LAND IN EUROPE. WE'RE ALMOST EXACTLY HALFWAY TO OUR ORIGINAL DESTINATION, SO I HOPE IT PUTS YOUR MINDS SOMEWHAT AT EASE THAT DUE TO THE CIRCUMSTANCES WE ARE RETURNING HOME... BACK TO CHICAGO.

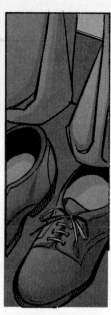

Clap

clap

clap

Clapp

Clappp

whew!

SORRY, FRIEND, BUT YOU'RE GOING TO WANT TO BE AWAKE FOR THIS.

HUH? WHAZZAT!?

IF WE'RE NOT CRASHIN', DON'T BOTHER ME.

HELLO?!?! HELLO??

IT'S NO USE! THE LINES ARE ALL *COMPLETELY* JAMMED UP.

≶SIGH≶

YEAH, MINE TOO.

BUT WHERE THERE'S A WILL, THERE'S A WAY.

I CAN'T LET YOU DO THIS.

LISTEN, BEAUTIFUL HATTIE, ARE WE OR ARE WE NOT LOOKING AT THE END OF THE WORLD AS WE KNOW IT?

DON'T PATRONIZE ME, SIR. I CAN'T LET YOU SIT HERE AND VANDALIZE AIRLINE PROPERTY.

I'M NOT VANDALIZING IT. I'M *ADAPTING* IT TO AN EMERGENCY. WITH THIS I CAN HOPEFULLY MAKE A CONNECTION WHERE NOTHING ELSE WILL WORK.

I CAN'T LET YOU DO THIS. DON'T MAKE ME BOTHER THE PILOT WITH THIS.

WOULDN'T YOU LIKE TO MAKE CONTACT WITH SOMEONE? IF THIS WORKS, I CAN REACH PEOPLE WHO CAN MAKE PHONE CALLS FOR YOU, LET YOUR FAMILY KNOW YOU'RE ALL RIGHT.

PLUS, I PROMISE I CAN PUT IT BACK THE WAY I FOUND IT.

WELL, I...I...

DEAL.

YOU'RE DOING THE RIGHT THING, HATTIE. IT'S OKAY IN A SITUATION LIKE THIS TO THINK OF YOURSELF A LITTLE.

BESIDES, YOU HAVE TO ADMIT, WHEN PEOPLE DISAPPEAR, SOME RULES GO OUT THE WINDOW.

Tackataka takatack

LATER...

ANY LUCK, MR. WILLIAMS?

Tackataka, takatack

SORRY, HATTIE.

WELL, THANKS FOR TRYING.

SO WHAT ARE YOU DOING?

WORKING ON MY STORY, JUST IN CASE I EVER *DO* CONNECT.

MAKE SURE TO TELL THEM ABOUT THE CHILDREN.

Tackataka, takatack

THE *CHILDREN?*

WE LOST SEVERAL OLD PEOPLE, BUT NOT *ALL* OF THEM. WE LOST SEVERAL MIDDLE-AGED PEOPLE, BUT NOT ALL OF THEM. AND WE LOST SEVERAL PEOPLE YOUR AGE AND MY AGE, BUT NOT *ALL* OF THEM. WE EVEN LOST SOME TEENAGERS.

BUT *EVERY SINGLE CHILD* AND BABY IS MISSING FROM THE PLANE.

THIS IS CAPTAIN STEELE. PLEASE MAKE SURE SEAT BELTS ARE FASTENED AND SECURE AS WE BEGIN OUR DESCENT INTO CHICAGO O'HARE.

THERE! THERE'S THE RUNWAY! IN ANOTHER FEW SECONDS WE'LL BE THROUGH THIS CLOUD COVER.

COVER SEEMS A BIT LOW, WOULDN'T YOU SAY, CAPTAIN?

I DON'T THINK THESE ARE CLOUDS, CHRIS...

WHAT ON EARTH?

IT'S SMOKE.

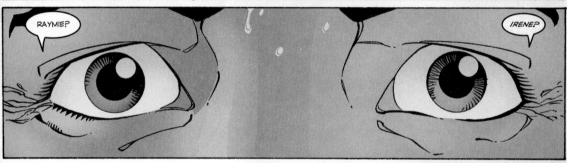

RAYMIE?

IRENE?

THIS IS A *DISASTER!* IN MY WILDEST NIGHTMARES, I... I COULDN'T IMAGINE ANYTHING WORSE THAN THIS! COULD YOU, CAPTAIN?

"ACTUALLY, CHRIS,
I *COULD*.

"SOMETHING MUCH,
MUCH WORSE..."

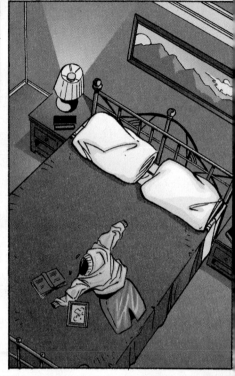

TO BE CONTINUED...